'Don't let fear hold you back.
You're **braver** than you think!'

Join Kitty for an enchanting
adventure by the light of the moon.

Kitty can talk to animals and
has feline superpowers.

Meet Kitty & her Cat Crew

Kitty

Kitty has special powers but is she ready to be a superhero just like her mum?

Luckily Kitty's Cat Crew have faith in her and show Kitty the hero that lies within!

Pumpkin

A stray ginger kitten who is utterly devoted to Kitty.

Figaro

Excitable and ready for adventure, Figaro knows
the neighbourhood like the back of his paw.

Pixie

Pixie has a nose for trouble
and a very active imagination!

Katsumi

Sleek and sophisticated,
Katsumi is quick to call Kitty
at the first sign of trouble.

For Kathy - P.H.

For Big and Little Red - J.L.

OXFORD
UNIVERSITY PRESS

Great Clarendon Street, Oxford OX2 6DP
Oxford University Press is a department of the University of Oxford.
It furthers the University's objective of excellence in research, scholarship,
and education by publishing worldwide. Oxford is a registered trade mark
of Oxford University Press in the UK and in certain other countries

British Library Cataloguing in Publication Data

Data available

ISBN: 978-0-19-277787-4

1 3 5 7 9 10 8 6 4 2

Printed in China

Paper used in the production of this book is a natural,
recyclable product made from wood grown in sustainable forests.
The manufacturing process conforms to the environmental
regulations of the country of origin.

Kitty

and the
Star Stone Robber

OXFORD
UNIVERSITY PRESS

Chapter 1

Kitty gazed around the Hallam City Museum with wide eyes. She had been looking forward to the school trip all week. There were so many amazing things to see, from tall stone statues to silver armour that gleamed in the sunlight pouring through the museum's glass dome roof.

'This way, everyone!' called Mrs Phillips, their teacher, and the class followed her up the grand marble staircase to the top floor.

The children chattered with excitement. They walked past a case containing triceratops bones and fossilized stegosaurus footprints. There were displays of jewel-like beetles, and drawings of parrots with rainbow-coloured wings.

Mrs Phillips clapped her hands. 'All right, everybody! You've got your pencils and rubbers, haven't you? Find one thing that you like and draw it carefully on your sheet. Don't forget to write down what it is.'

Lots of children rushed towards the triceratops bones.

Kitty walked along looking at all the exhibits. At last, she stopped by the rocks and crystals display and leaned closer. Dozens of brightly coloured stones lay in the case. In one corner, there was a rock speckled with silver and amber jewels that winked and sparkled in the light.

Kitty read the label: *This meteorite was found on Jamal's Hill. Meteorites are rocks that fall to Earth from Outer*

Space. She smiled. This stone had come a very long way! Taking out her pencil, she began drawing the meteorite on her piece of paper. She couldn't wait to tell her kitten, Pumpkin, all about it when she got home.

That evening, Kitty sat on the roof
terrace outside her bedroom window.
Pumpkin snuggled up beside her.
Hundreds of stars glittered in the
dark sky and a bright full moon was
rising over the rooftops.

'This was my favourite thing
in the whole museum, Pumpkin.'
Kitty showed the ginger kitten
her drawing.

'It's a rock from Outer Space—
like a stone that fell from the stars!'

'Ooh, it sounds magical!' meowed
Pumpkin.

Kitty smiled. She loved sharing
things with Pumpkin. She was a
superhero-in-training and the best part
of her cat-like superpowers was being
able to talk to animals. She'd met
Pumpkin on her very first mission and
they had been best friends ever since!

Kitty's powers let her leap and run
and balance as gracefully as a cat, and

she often went on moonlit adventures
across the city rooftops with her cat
crew. Her super senses let her hear
and see things easily in the dark.

Kitty's mum, who was a
superhero herself, climbed out onto
the terrace in her catsuit. 'Goodnight,
Kitty! I'm going to work now
and Dad is reading your brother
a bedtime story.' She smiled and
smoothed Kitty's hair gently. 'Don't
forget to put on your cape if you go
out on an adventure.'

'I won't! Night, Mum.'

Kitty hugged her.

across to the next rooftop and raced

away into the dark. Kitty watched her

disappearing into the distance.

'I suppose we should go to bed

then,' said Pumpkin with a yawn.

Kitty stretched her arms, feeling her superpowers tingling inside her. The moon was full and bright, and she felt like running and jumping, not going to bed.

'Maybe we could stay outside a bit longer,' she said to Pumpkin. 'I feel excited—as if there's an adventure waiting to happen!' She climbed to the top of the roof and somersaulted over the chimney pot.

'Kitty, are you there?' called a familiar voice.

Kitty caught sight of Figaro trotting across the rooftops. Moonlight flashed on the white tip of his tail. 'Hi, Figaro!' she called. 'Have you come to play with us?'

'I dashed here as fast as I could. I'm dreadfully worried, Kitty!' Figaro gasped, leaping onto the roof terrace. 'There's a wriggly feeling in my stomach and my whiskers won't stop trembling.'

'Oh dear!' said Pumpkin. 'Did you eat too much mackerel again?'

'Absolutely not! I ate just the right amount.' Figaro licked his whiskers.

'No, I'm worried about the treasures at the City Museum. I saw a creature creeping about inside when I passed by just now.'

'It was probably Cleo the security cat,' said Kitty.

'I don't think so!' Figaro replied. 'They were much larger than Cleo with funny sticking-up ears. I couldn't see very well because they disappeared behind a suit of armour, but I'm certain they were not meant to be there. What if we wake up tomorrow and every

single treasure in the museum
is gone?'

Kitty frowned. It did
sound suspicious. 'Let's go to
the museum right now and
investigate. I'll just put my
superhero outfit on!' Climbing
through the open window, she
quickly put on her mask and tied
her cape around her neck.

As she leapt back onto the roof,
Kitty's cape billowed out in the
wind. Energy buzzed inside her and
she turned a row of cartwheels
across the rooftop.

'Wait for me, Kitty!' cried Pumpkin, scampering after her.

The moon shone brightly as they hurried towards Crown Street where the museum stood. Its huge glass roof towered above the city, glittering in the moonlight.

Kitty stopped on the roof opposite and used her special night

vision to look inside. Everything seemed quiet. There was a light on in the security guard's office on the ground floor, but nothing was moving.

'There's no one there!' Pumpkin said, yawning. 'Maybe you imagined it?'

'There *was* someone in there,' Figaro insisted. 'I watched them sneaking about.'

Kitty curled her hair behind her ear, listening carefully. All her super senses were on high alert and her skin prickled. She had a funny feeling that something was wrong.

Then she spotted a shadow moving on the top floor. A dark shape slipped past the museum window and disappeared again.

'You're right! There's someone in

there,' Kitty whispered. 'I'm going to get closer.'

Swinging across to a lamppost, Kitty made a huge leap and landed on a high window ledge. Climbing quickly, she reached the top floor and peered through the museum window.

A shadow was moving near the triceratops bones. Kitty caught her breath. Who was that—sneaking around in the dark? She leaned closer—trying to see—but moonlight reflected off the glass right into her eyes.

She blinked and felt around
for the window catch. Pushing the
window open, she leapt swiftly
into the dark museum.

Chapter 2

The top floor of the museum
was silent and still. Moonlight gleamed
on the glass case with the triceratops
bones. Kitty looked around for the
shape she'd seen moving in the dark.
She was certain the intruder was still

here, hiding in the shadows.

Stopping beside the triceratops
display, she found grubby paw marks
smeared across the glass. The case was
open at one end and some of the bones
were missing.

Suddenly a voice yowled, 'WHO'S THERE? Come out right now!'

Kitty jumped. Then she recognized Cleo, the museum security cat, bounding up the stairs.

Cleo stopped in front of Kitty, her fur on end. 'What's going on? Was it you making a noise just now?'

Kitty put a finger to her lips, whispering, 'No, there's someone else here! Look, they've stolen some of the dinosaur bones.'

'How dare they!' Cleo scowled. 'They won't get away with it! Shh, what was that?'

Kitty held her breath, listening very carefully. There was a faint scratching sound in the corner of the room. Creeping forwards, she edged around the display cases.

The scratching stopped.

Cleo signalled to Kitty and crept towards the door. Kitty understood at once. Between them, they could corner the robber before they escaped!

The scratching started up again and Kitty tiptoed closer, using her night vision to peer through the shadows.

'Gotcha!' cried Cleo, switching on the light.

Kitty stared down at a tiny mouse scuttling underneath the cabinets.

This couldn't be the thief. The creature wasn't big enough to lift a dinosaur bone.

Suddenly she saw a huge four-legged shadow moving on the staircase wall. The shadow had sticking-out ears and a thick tail, and they were holding a bulging bag in their jaws. The robber had managed to slip past them and was sneaking away down the stairs.

'Cleo, look behind you!' shouted Kitty.

The robber fled down the steps, their claws clattering as they ran. Kitty

gave chase, leaping down the stairs
two at a time, and Cleo galloped
after her.

The thief dashed into the soldier
exhibition on the bottom floor.

Kitty darted past rows
of shields and tall suits
of armour.

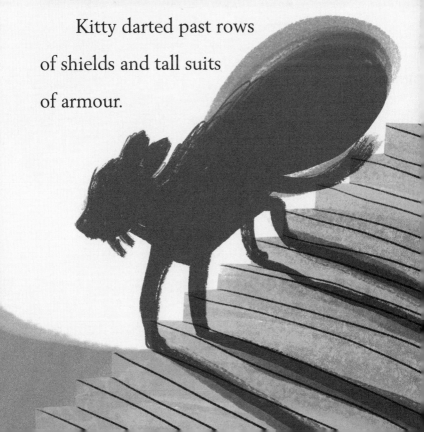

She tried to get a good look at the thief but every time she got closer, they dodged away behind a statue.

'Stop right there!' Cleo shouted. 'How dare you steal from MY museum?'

The thief chuckled and ran past the ticket office. Kitty leapt over the turnstiles and ran after them. The robber flung something into the air and Kitty ducked. She stopped to look as the object rolled away across the floor. It was a stone from the crystal display upstairs.

34

The thief disappeared around a corner. Kitty raced after them, but all she found was an open window at the end of an empty corridor. Climbing through the window, she jumped out onto the path below.

'Kitty, what happened?' Figaro ran over to meet her with Pumpkin close behind.

'Did you see the thief? Which way did he go?' gasped Kitty, looking all around.

'We didn't see him,' said Pumpkin,

wide-eyed. 'He must have got away.'

Kitty shinned up a lamppost to get a better view. The museum stood near a crossroads, and streets and alleyways led off in every direction. Something moved on the other side of the road, but it was just a crisp packet blowing along in the wind.

Cleo leaned out of the museum window, her whiskers twitching.

'That thief had a strange smell—like onions and gravy.'

'Maybe they live near a restaurant,' suggested Figaro. 'I've often thought of moving closer to the fishmongers. If I can persuade my humans, of course.'

'I'm going back upstairs to check what's missing,' Cleo said gloomily. 'Stan, the guard, is going to be so cross when he finally wakes up from his nap.'

'We'll come with you and look for clues.' Kitty leapt back inside and Figaro and Pumpkin followed.

While Cleo checked each exhibit, Kitty examined the paw marks on the triceratops display. They were smudged so it was impossible to tell what kind of animal had made them.

'The robber's taken all the prettiest stones from the rock cabinet,' Cleo said crossly. 'It's such a greedy thing to do!'

Kitty joined Cleo beside the glass case. The beautiful star stone she had drawn earlier that day had vanished, along with a handful of other jewels. Kitty stared at the empty space in the display. It was so sad that other visitors wouldn't be able to look at the beautiful silver and amber stone.

'I can see why the thief wanted those pretty jewels,' said Figaro. 'But why did they bother with the smelly old dinosaur bones?'

Kitty rubbed her forehead. 'I don't know. I wish I knew who it was.'

Cleo sprang out from under the cabinet waving a black eye mask. 'The thief left this behind! Maybe it'll help us track them down.'

Kitty took the mask and examined it closely. 'Dodger wears a mask like this AND she loves stealing shiny things . . . the thief laughed as they ran away, which is just like Dodger too!'

'But Dodger doesn't like bones,'

Figaro pointed out. 'Are you sure it was her?'

'I didn't get a good look, but they definitely laughed like Dodger.' Kitty sighed as she tucked the mask into her pocket. Dodger was a clever thief who especially loved sparkly jewels, but lately, Kitty hoped she might be changing her naughty ways.

'I've heard all about Dodger,' said Cleo. 'She's a sneaky kind of cat and I know she's stolen things before. Doesn't she live in the Wonder Tower?'

Pumpkin nodded. 'Yes, in the restaurant on the top floor. She's probably hiding the stolen things there right now.'

Cleo frowned. 'She lives in the restaurant? Maybe that's why I caught the scent of onions and gravy.'

Kitty leapt forwards and turned a somersault, her superpowers buzzing inside her. 'We have to hurry! I'm going over there right now to get the jewels back again.'

Chapter 3

Cleo waved them all goodbye and went back inside to wait for Stan to wake up. Kitty, Pumpkin, and Figaro crossed the street and climbed a drainpipe to reach the rooftops. The full moon shone down, casting silvery light over the quiet city.

Kitty raced
towards the great glass
Wonder Tower which rose
majestically into the night sky. A little
red light winked on the radio mast at the
top of the tower. Leaping from roof to
roof, Kitty felt the wind whoosh
past her.

Figaro and Pumpkin ran after her
as fast as they could.

'Slow down, Kitty!' panted Figaro.
'Do we have to go so fast? It's not good
for my paws!'

'We've got to catch Dodger before
she hides those jewels!' Kitty sprang to
the next rooftop. Then, climbing down
to a windowsill, she leapt gracefully to
the ground.

The Wonder Tower loomed
over them like a huge grey giant and
moonlight glittered on its hundreds of

windows. Lights were on in the Cloud Restaurant on the top floor.

Kitty dashed towards the main entrance, her cape flying out behind her. She was determined to find Dodger and make her return everything she'd stolen. Then she would take the star stone back to Cleo again.

Dashing into the lift, Kitty waited for Figaro and Pumpkin before pressing the button for the top floor. The lift whizzed past a hundred and twenty floors and then stopped. The doors pinged open.

Kitty tiptoed through the restaurant door. Maybe, if she sneaked inside really quietly, she could catch Dodger hiding the jewels.

'Hi there, Kitty!' Dodger called cheerily. 'I saw you coming over the rooftops. Have you come to try my fish and mango smoothie at last?'

The cheeky cat was stretched lazily across the top of a grand piano. She flicked her tail and, when she smiled, her teeth gleamed like diamonds. Beside her was a plate piled high with salmon and a tall glass filled with her famous smoothie.

Figaro spotted the salmon and his whiskers started twitching.

Kitty put her hands on her hips.

'Where are the jewels and the dinosaur bones, Dodger? You can't just take things from the museum like that. Those treasures are for everyone to see.'

Dodger licked a paw and smoothed her fur. 'I don't know what you're talking about. I haven't been anywhere near the museum.' She leaned over and started playing the piano with one paw.

Kitty pulled the eye mask from her pocket. 'This is yours, isn't it? We found it on the floor of the museum and that proves you were there!'

Dodger frowned and banged the piano keys. 'I told you! I haven't been there tonight.'

'It must have been you!' cried Kitty.

'I heard you laugh.'

'So you came all the way here
to accuse me of stealing? Silly me for
thinking you'd come to visit a friend!'
Dodger sprang onto the piano stool
and started thumping the keys with
both paws.

Kitty stared around. Where would
Dodger have hidden everything?

Crouching down, she peered under the restaurant tables. Then she dashed over to the piano and opened the lid, but there were no jewels hidden inside.

Figaro leapt forwards and caught the plate of salmon before it tumbled to the floor.

Dodger leapt off the piano stool, her eyes flashing. 'There's nothing here! I told you—I haven't stolen anything.'

'Maybe the thief was someone else, Kitty,' Pumpkin said.

Kitty hesitated. She had been so

sure it was Dodger. But what if she was wrong?

Dodger grabbed the eye mask out of Kitty's fingers and scampered to the door. 'I can see you still don't believe me!' she snapped. 'So I'm going to catch the thief myself. And then you can say you're sorry!'

'Dodger, wait!' said Kitty.

'Can I finish off your salmon?' Figaro called after her.

But Dodger had gone, leaving the door swinging behind her.

Kitty's heart sank. She'd never seen Dodger look so upset before.

'I don't think she did take those things from the museum, Kitty,' said Pumpkin. 'She sounded really sure about it and there's nothing to prove that the eye mask was actually hers.'

'Oh dear! I think you might be right.' Kitty raced after Dodger but the lift doors had already closed.

Kitty, Pumpkin, and Figaro headed to the bottom of the Wonder Tower and searched the street for Dodger, but the other cat had vanished.

Kitty had an awful feeling in her tummy. 'I just wanted to get the museum treasures back for Cleo. I didn't mean to hurt Dodger's feelings.'

'And the real thief is still out there somewhere,' Figaro pointed out. 'They probably think they've got away with it too.'

Kitty straightened her cat ears, thinking carefully. 'Figaro, could you take Pumpkin home? It's getting quite late . . . and if you see anyone from our cat crew tell them to look out for a robber with a loot bag. I'm going back to the museum to look for more clues.'

'Good luck!' mewed Figaro, as he and Pumpkin headed down the street.

* * *

Back in the museum, Kitty searched carefully for more clues. She found more paw prints near the rocks and crystals cabinet. They looked quite big—too big to be Dodger's. In fact, they didn't look like cat's paw marks at all.

Cleo sighed as she padded across the museum. 'I've checked the whole building and there's nothing else missing. Did you find anything, Kitty?'

Kitty shook her head. 'The thief wasn't Dodger. I'm looking for more clues.'

There was a tap at the window and a furry white face peered through the glass.

'Pixie! What are you doing here?' Kitty let her friend inside.

Pixie sprang down from the windowsill. Her fluffy white coat stood on end. 'I heard about the robbery from Figaro and Pumpkin, so I came straight over here . . . and on the way something awful happened!'

'Oh no! Are you all right?' asked Kitty.

'I'm OK but Dodger's in trouble! I could hear her yowling for miles,' Pixie explained.

'What's wrong—is she hurt?' Kitty's eyes widened.

'I'm not sure. She could be hurt or lost or maybe something with really big teeth was chasing her!' Pixie gulped. 'I've never heard anyone screech so loudly.'

'We'd better hurry!' cried Kitty. 'I'm sorry, Cleo. I've got to go! I think Dodger needs me.' She leapt onto the windowsill and bounded out into the moonlit night.

Chapter 4

Kitty's heart thumped as she followed Pixie down the shadowy street. Her stomach turned over as she remembered what Dodger had said before she ran away: *I'm going to catch the thief myself. And then you can say*

you're sorry!

Dodger had only left the Wonder Tower because Kitty had accused her of stealing from the museum. If Dodger got hurt, it would be all her fault!

'Where did you hear all the noise, Pixie?' Kitty asked anxiously.

'Just around this corner,' Pixie replied. 'I could hear Dodger shouting and mewing. Then I ran away to find you as fast as I could.'

Kitty stopped and listened carefully. The wind whooshed down the street, making her dark hair flutter. Slowly, her super senses began to work harder. Her night vision became clearer and her super hearing sharpened. She took a deep breath and caught the scent of fish and mango smoothie. There must be smears of it on Dodger's whiskers. That meant she could be quite close by!

'Pixie, this way!' Kitty followed the scent to the house on the corner. Creeping up the path, she peered through the living room window.

Inside, there was a brown sofa and

a round orange rug. Photos of Stan, the museum guard, hugging a brown-and-white dog hung on the wall.

Kitty frowned. This must be Stan's house. Why would Dodger come here? Stan would still be at the museum finishing his night shift.

A strange rattling noise came from inside the house.

Pixie's eyes widened. 'That sounds like a ghost! Maybe we should go, Kitty. This is way too scary.'

'Don't be frightened, Pixie!' Kitty

whispered. 'I'm sure Dodger's here somewhere. I can still smell the fish and mango smoothie she likes.'

Tiptoeing around the corner of the house, Kitty noticed the back door was slightly open. This time she caught the scent of onions and gravy. It was the same smell that Cleo had noticed in the museum—the scent of the thief.

Kitty peeped around the door. There was a plate on the table and a leftover sausage stew on top of the oven. She crept through the open door and gasped.

Dodger was trapped inside a large brown dog crate. Shaking the bars of the cage, she yowled angrily.

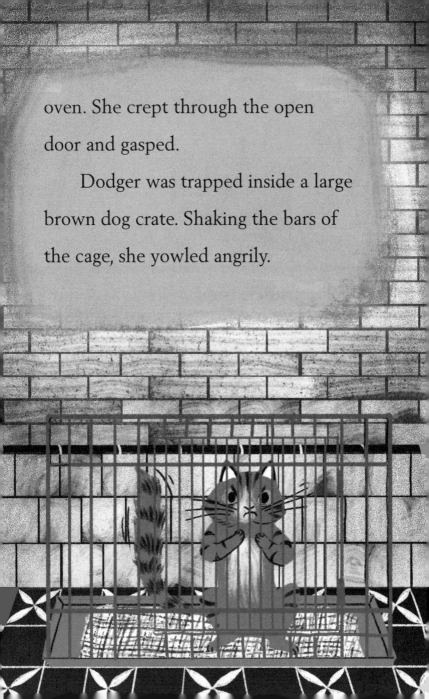

'Dodger, are you all right?' Kitty rushed over to the crate and tried to open the catch. It was rusty and stiff.

'Kitty, what are you doing here?' Dodger stared in surprise.

'Pixie heard you yelling, so I came looking for you,' Kitty explained. 'How did you end up in here?'

'It was that horrible dog!' hissed Dodger.

'What dog?' Pixie asked.

'That terrier—he was here just now!' Dodger stared around wildly.

Kitty gave the catch one more pull
and it flew open.

Dodger leapt out of the cage. Her
eyes were fierce and her fur stood on end.

'What happened?' Kitty asked again.
'Was the thief here?'

'I spotted him in an alleyway,'
meowed Dodger. 'He looked pretty
suspicious with his swag bag in his mouth,
but he disappeared as
soon as I started
following him.

I tracked him here, but as soon as I stepped inside the kitchen he pushed me into this cage and shut me in. How DARE he lock up the Great Dodger?'

Kitty took a deep breath. She knew she hadn't been fair to Dodger and she ought to apologize. 'I'm so sorry about what happened before. I should never have accused you of breaking into the museum.'

'There's no time for that!' cried Dodger. 'That dog is the museum thief. We have to find him right now!' She hurtled out of the back door and rushed across the yard into the street.

Kitty and Pixie ran after her. They caught up with Dodger on the corner by a patch of wasteland. A brown-and-white dog with a stubby tail was hastily digging a hole by some bushes. The moon disappeared behind a cloud and darkness spread across the wasteland.

'That's him!' hissed Dodger. 'He's acting pretty suspiciously, don't you think? I bet he's burying the stolen goods in that hole.'

'He must belong to Stan, the security guard at the museum,' whispered Kitty. 'I know that was Stan's house because I recognized his photo on the wall.'

'He can't be a very good guard if he lets his dog steal from the museum,' Dodger whispered back.

Pixie suddenly sneezed.

The dog spun around, his ears pricked.

Kitty ducked behind a
bush, pulling Pixie and Dodger
with her. The dog turned around
again and began to dig even
faster. Lumps of earth flew into
the air as his hole grew deeper
and deeper.

'Maybe we should just go and talk to him,' Kitty said worriedly. 'We don't really know if he stole those things. I don't want to blame the wrong person again.'

'I saw him with a loot bag,' insisted Dodger. 'Why don't you believe me, Kitty?'

'I do believe you! But I only saw his shadow before and it didn't look like a dog's.' Kitty rubbed her forehead. Could this really be the robber from the museum with his sticking-out ears

and thick tail?

Suddenly the moon sailed out from behind the clouds. The dog's shadow grew tall and dark in the bright moonlight.

Kitty caught her breath. It was the same shadow she'd seen on the museum wall. 'You're right—that's him! Quick, get him before he escapes again.'

Treading softly, Kitty and her friends crept towards the thief.

The dog dropped something into the hole and began covering it with earth and stones. Kitty caught a glimpse of something black beneath his paws. Was that the loot bag with the jewels inside?

Kitty tiptoed closer. Then she

crouched down, ready to pounce.
Dodger sneaked through the bushes
and Pixie dodged behind a tree. The
terrier went on filling the hole and
scattering earth everywhere with his
paws.

Suddenly, Kitty leapt out of her
hiding place and caught the dog by his
collar. 'Hey, wait! What are you putting
in that hole?'

'A-ROOOO!' The dog howled and
tried to shake Kitty off.

Dodger jumped out in front of

him, her green eyes gleaming. 'Stop right there, Mr Sticky Paws! I know you took those things from the museum. You'd better give them back right now!'

'I don't know what you're talking about,' barked the dog.

'What museum? I don't know anything about a museum.'

'Your owner works there,' said Kitty. 'I saw the photos of you and Stan on the wall of your house.'

'What house? You've got the wrong animal!' The dog wriggled and writhed, and Kitty struggled to hold on to his collar.

'Quick, Pixie!' she called to her friend. 'Find out what he was burying.'

Pixie bounced forwards.
Then she peered into the hole
and shuddered. 'It's all very
muddy in there!'

'Oh, just let me do it!' Dodger leapt into the hollow and started digging fiercely.

Earth splattered all over Pixie's white fur and she jumped out of the way with a disgusted mew. Dodger dug deeper and deeper. There, at the bottom of the hole, lay a large black bag.

The dog broke free from Kitty's grasp and made a desperate lunge for the bag, but Dodger snatched it out of the way just in time.

'Open it, Dodger!' cried Kitty. 'Let's see what's inside.'

Chapter 5

Dodger tipped the loot bag upside down and a pile of jewels and dinosaur bones poured out. The precious stones sparkled in the moonlight and the star stone with its silver and amber jewels shone brightest of all.

'Ooh, that's so pretty!' cried Pixie.

'You DID take the things from
the museum!' Kitty said to the dog.
'Why did you do it? You could get your
owner, Stan, into a lot of trouble. What
if someone thought he'd taken all these
things himself?'

The dog hung his head. 'I didn't really think of that.'

'What's your name?' Kitty asked. 'I suppose Stan doesn't know what you've been doing?'

'I'm Magnus,' the terrier told them. 'I decided to take the bones after Stan told me about the dinosaur display at the museum. I love old bones! Then last night I saw those pretty jewels and I wanted those too.'

Dodger picked up the star stone and turned it over. 'They're very pretty but you should never take things that aren't yours. It's VERY wrong!' She winked at Kitty.

'Why don't you help us take these treasures back to the museum?' Kitty said to Magnus. 'We can give them to Cleo, the museum cat, and then your owner won't get in trouble.' She gathered the bones and jewels into the bag again and tied the strings.

'Give them back—they're mine!' Magnus burst into wild yapping and Pixie hid behind Kitty's legs.

'You can't keep them,' Kitty said firmly.
'They belong to the museum.'

'Not any more!' barked Magnus.
'They're mine and I'm keeping them for
ever.' Grabbing the bag with his teeth, he
galloped away into the dark.

'Don't let him escape!' squeaked Pixie.

Dodger gave chase with Kitty and Pixie
close behind. Magnus rushed away from the
wasteland and fled down the street.

'Get back here, thief!' shouted

Dodger, her eyes gleaming.

Magnus hurtled past a row of shops and stopped at the corner. He spun round to check whether Kitty was following, before disappearing into a dark alleyway.

'We can still catch him,' Kitty said, breathlessly. 'Follow me!'

'We're coming, Kitty!' cried Pixie.

Kitty pumped her arms and legs, running faster than ever. Little by little, she drew closer to the robber dog.

Halfway along the alley, Magnus kicked over a row of dustbins. A huge

crash echoed up and down the passage as they tumbled over one by one. The bins rolled around, blocking the alleyway while Magnus galloped away into the distance.

'Come back you naughty dog!' howled Dodger.

'Pixie! Dodger! Help me.' Kitty pushed the bins out of the way and raced after the dog.

But when they reached the end of the alley, the next street was empty.

'Now what do we do?' grumbled Dodger.

Kitty scanned the shadowy street. Magnus had to be somewhere close by. 'We can find him if we work together. Pixie, you stand here and keep a lookout. If you see him give a loud meow! Dodger, you climb that tree and be ready to jump down when I give the signal.'

'Where are you going, Kitty?' asked Pixie.

'Up to the rooftops!' Kitty shinned up a drainpipe, whispering back, 'Remember, stay quiet! He's probably hiding somewhere, but he won't be able to hide for ever.'

The wind whooshed down
the street, blowing leaves along the
pavement. Kitty sprang along the
rooftops with her cape rippling in the
breeze. She stopped, listening for sounds
from the pavement below, but all she
heard was the distant rattle of a train.

Using her night vision, she looked
up and down the street. Suddenly, she
heard a faint scratching noise from
underneath a parked car. A furry face with
a brown nose poked out from behind the
back wheel. Then Magnus slipped out of
his hiding place and made off down the
street, dragging his loot bag with him.

Kitty waved to Dodger,
who leapt down from the tree.
Running along the rooftops, Kitty
kept pace with the escaping
dog. Her superpowers tingled
through her body. She swung
down to a window ledge. Then
she somersaulted high into the air
and landed on top of a wall.

Dodger almost caught up with the robber dog, but Magnus turned and snapped at her. Dodger fell back and Magnus raced away at top speed.

Kitty leapt onto the roof of a parked car and jumped from one car to the next. Somersaulting to the ground, she grabbed the loot bag out of the dog's paws.

'Give that back—it's mine!' growled Magnus.

'These treasures belong to the museum and I'm taking them back right now,' said Kitty, firmly. 'I think I ought to tell your owner that you stole them too.'

'Don't tell Stan!' whined Magnus. 'I don't want him to think I'm a naughty dog.'

Kitty frowned. 'But if I don't tell him, will you promise never to take things from the museum again?'

'Yes, yes! I promise,' Magnus said eagerly.

Pixie twitched her whiskers. 'I don't believe you! You don't look very

98

sorry to me.'

Kitty hesitated. Pixie was right. Magnus didn't look sorry. He only seemed worried about getting caught. What if he decided to steal again? She had to make sure the treasures at the museum would be safe from now on.

'I have an idea,' she told Magnus. 'Come with me. There's something I need to show you!'

Chapter 6

The museum building stood quiet and still in the moonlight. Kitty lifted Magnus through the ground floor window. Then Pixie

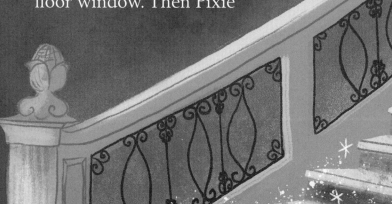

and Dodger leapt inside and
they all hurried down the
corridor to the grand marble
staircase.

Their shadows stretched
up the staircase wall.

Kitty looked at Magnus's shadow, with its big ears and round nose, and wondered how she had ever thought it might be Dodger!

The moon came out from behind a cloud as they reached the top floor. Pale light poured through the great glass dome, turning everything silver. Kitty stopped by the triceratops case and untied the loot bag.

Taking out the dinosaur bones, she placed them carefully back where they belonged. 'There's something I want to show you,' she told Magnus.

The terrier trotted after her as she walked over to the rocks and crystals display. Kitty took the star stone from the loot bag and read out the description in the display case.

'This is a meteorite that came from the stars!' she explained. 'It's a shooting star and it's thousands of years old. It came all the way from a distant galaxy.'

Magnus listened as Kitty read out information about each of the stones. He wagged his tail and his eyes grew bright. 'Wow, that's amazing! I never knew these jewels were so interesting.'

'They are!' Kitty smiled. 'And if they

stay here at the museum then everyone
in the whole city can learn about them.'

Magnus frowned. 'I guess so . . .'

'After all, what's the use of taking
these jewels if you have to hide them
away?' Kitty went on. 'Isn't it better if
everyone has the chance to see them?'

'You're right! I'm sorry, Kitty,'
said Magnus. 'I've been really selfish.
What can I do to make up for what I've
done?'

Cleo marched into the room,
looking stern. 'You can start by

helping clean up the mess you made downstairs. You knocked over a wooden carving and there's dust everywhere. There's a lot of sweeping to do.'

'I'll get started right away!' Magnus said eagerly.

'And THEN you can do some dusting and some tidying up, and THEN you can help me count all the new exhibits . . .' Cleo carried on listing more and more jobs as she led Magnus away.

Dodger stretched out with a purr. 'That's another mission completed then, Kitty. I guess you needed some help this time. You really couldn't have done it without me!'

'You needed Kitty to break open that dog crate,' Pixie pointed out. 'You'd still be stuck in there if she hadn't rescued you.'

'I only ended up in there because I was trying to prove I was innocent!' Dodger flicked her tail and looked offended.

Kitty knelt down beside Dodger.

'I'm really sorry I thought you were the thief! I should have believed you right away when you said it wasn't you.'

Dodger stuck her nose in the air. 'I TOLD you I didn't know anything about the robbery. I have been SUCH a good cat lately.'

'I'm very sorry!' Kitty held out her hand. 'I know I hurt your feelings. You will forgive me, won't you, Dodger?'

Dodger gave a sniff and her green
eyes flashed. Then she grinned and put
her paw in Kitty's hand. 'Of course
I will! It was fun tracking down the
real thief and I want to try out that
somersault move you did, Kitty. It
looked awesome!'

Kitty put the rest of the stones
back into the rock cabinet and closed
the case. The bright jewels on the star
stone glittered in the moonlight.

'It's a shame we can't just keep
ONE jewel,' said Dodger, peering at the

star stone. 'This one's very pretty.'

'Dodger!' laughed Kitty. 'I thought you were being a good cat?'

Dodger gave a wink and a wave before darting out of the window into the night.

Carrying Pixie on her shoulder,
Kitty climbed onto the museum roof
and gazed out over the rooftops.
Stars gleamed in the night sky and
thousands of tiny street lights glittered
across the city below.

Kitty smiled at Pixie. 'Shall we find

Pumpkin and Figaro and tell them all about our adventure?'

'Good idea!' agreed Pixie. 'Look, Kitty! What's that?'

Kitty looked up and spotted a beautiful twinkly light zooming across the sky. 'It's a meteor just like the one we saved tonight,' she said.

'A star stone!' meowed Pixie. 'Maybe it's a sign of good luck.'

'Maybe!' Kitty nodded. 'And with good friends like you and Dodger, I feel very lucky indeed.'

Super Facts About Cats

Super Speed

Have you ever seen a cat make a quick escape from a dog? If so, you'll know that they can move *really* fast—up to 30mph!

Super Hearing

Cats have an incredible sense of hearing and can swivel their large ears to pinpoint even the tiniest of sounds.

Super Reflexes

Have you ever heard the saying 'cats always land on their feet'? People say this because cats have amazing reflexes. If a cat is falling, they can sense quickly how to move their bodies into the right position to land safely.

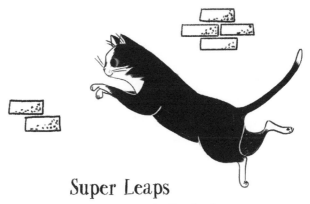

Super Leaps

A cat can jump over eight feet high
in a single leap; this is due to its powerful
back leg muscles.

Super Vision

Cats have amazing night-time vision. Their
incredible ability to see in low light allows them
to hunt for prey when it's dark outside.

Super Smell

Cats have a very powerful sense of smell,
14 times stronger than a human's. Did you know
that the pattern of ridges on each cat's nose
is as unique as a human's fingerprint?

About the author

Paula Harrison

Before launching a successful writing career,
Paula was a primary school teacher. Her years teaching
taught her what children like in stories and how
they respond to humour and suspense. She went on
to put her experience to good use, writing many
successful stories for young readers.

About the illustrator

Jenny Løvlie

Jenny is a Norwegian illustrator, designer,
creative, foodie, and bird enthusiast. She is fascinated
by the strong bond between humans and animals and
loves using bold colours and shapes in her work.

Love Kitty?
Why not try these too . . .

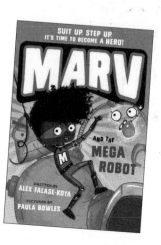